72-BIB-591

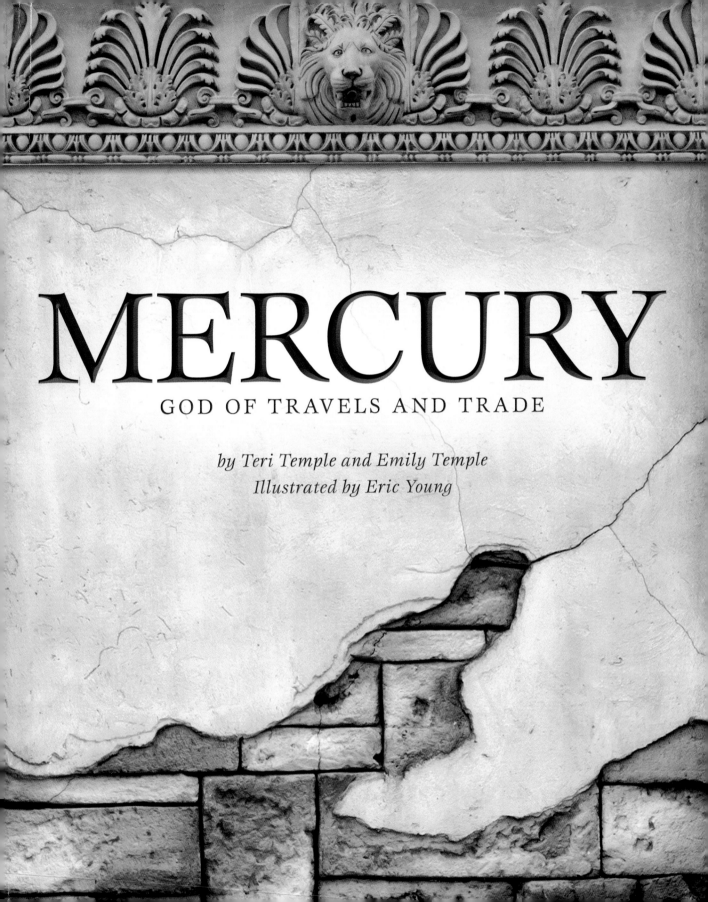

MERCURY

GOD OF TRAVELS AND TRADE

by Teri Temple and Emily Temple
Illustrated by Eric Young

Published by The Child's World®
1980 Lookout Drive • Mankato, MN 56003-1705
800-599-READ • www.childsworld.com

ACKNOWLEDGMENTS
The Child's World®: Mary Berendes, Publishing Director
Red Line Editorial: Editorial direction
The Design Lab: Design and production
Design elements ©: Banana Republic Images/Shutterstock Images; Shutterstock
Images; Anton Balazh/Shutterstock Images
Photographs ©: Viacheslav Lopatin/Shutterstock Images, 5; Bettmann/Corbis,
12; Shutterstock Images, 15, 16, 28; NASA, 27

ISBN 9781631437205
LCCN 2014945432

Printed in the United States of America
Mankato, MN
November, 2014
PA02241

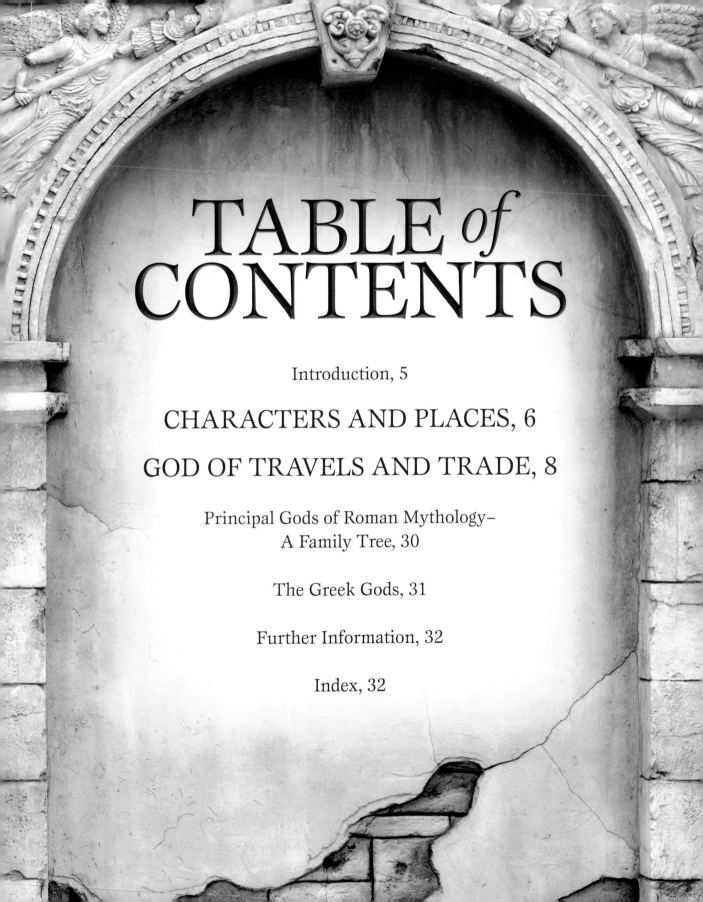

TABLE *of* CONTENTS

INTRODUCTION

In ancient times Romans believed in spirits or gods called numina. In Latin, *numina* means divine will or power. The Romans took part in religious rituals to please the gods. They felt the gods had powers that could make their lives better.

As the Roman government grew more powerful, its armies conquered many neighboring lands. Romans often adopted beliefs from these new cultures. They greatly admired the Greek arts and sciences. Gradually, the Romans combined the Greek myths and religion with their own. These stories shaped and influenced each part of a Roman citizen's daily life. Ancient Roman poets, such as Ovid and Virgil, wrote down these tales of wonder. Their writings became a part of Rome's great history. To the Romans, however, these stories were not just for entertainment. Roman mythology was their key to understanding the world.

ANCIENT ROMAN SOCIETIES
Ancient Roman society was divided into several groups. The patricians were the most powerful and wealthiest group. They often owned land and held power in the government. The plebeians worked for the patricians. Slaves were prisoners of war or children without parents. Some slaves were freed and enjoyed most of the rights of citizens.

CHARACTERS AND PLACES

ANCIENT ROME

ADRIATIC SEA

ROME

TYRRHENIAN SEA

OLYMPIAN GODS (*uh-LIM-pee-uhn*)**:**
*Ceres with daughter Proserpine, Mercury,
Vulcan, Venus with son Cupid, Mars, Juno,
Jupiter, Neptune, Minerva, Apollo, Diana,
Bacchus, Vesta, and Pluto*

UNDERWORLD: *The land of the dead;
ruled over by the god of the dead, Pluto; must
cross the River Styx to gain entrance*

APOLLO (*a-POL-lo*)

God of the Sun, music, healing, and prophecy; son of Jupiter and Latona; twin to Diana

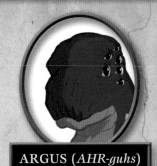

ARGUS (*AHR-guhs*)

A monster with 100 eyes; Juno's servant

FAUNUS (*FAW-nuhs*)

God of nature; son of Mercury; has the legs, horns, and tail of a goat

GRAY SISTERS

Guardians of the Gorgons; shared one eye and one tooth among them

JUNO (*JOO-noh*)

Queen of the gods; married to Jupiter

JUPITER (*JOO-pi-ter*)

Supreme ruler of the heavens and of the gods on Mount Olympus; son of Saturn and Ops; married to Juno; father of many gods and heroes

MAIA (*MEY-yeh*)

Goddess of spring; mother of Mercury

MERCURY (*MUR-kyuh-ree*)

Messenger to the gods; god of trade; son of Jupiter

PERSEUS (*PUR-see-uhs*)

Hero who killed Medusa; married to Andromeda

GOD OF TRAVELS AND TRADE

The Roman god Mercury was very merry and clever. This helped him secure a spot as one of the 12 Olympian gods. These gods lived on Mount Olympus in a beautiful palace. Mercury's tale began with his father's wandering nature.

Mercury's father, Jupiter, was the king of the gods. He was the supreme ruler of heaven and Earth. Jupiter ruled over Mount Olympus with his wife, Juno. Juno was beautiful. She was also very jealous. Jupiter had other wives, and Juno did not like to share him. Juno often punished the women Jupiter met with. So Jupiter often sneaked behind Juno's back to see maidens on Earth.

Mercury's mother, Maia, was one of these maidens. Maia was a lovely mountain nymph. Jupiter often sneaked out to visit Maia while Juno was asleep. Maia lived in a cave. The cave was so deep Juno never saw that Maia was pregnant. As a result, Maia delivered her and Jupiter's baby in peace.

Mercury was extremely smart, even as a baby. He understood things that were well ahead of his age. On the very first day of his life, he managed to cause mischief for the gods.

While his mother was sleeping, baby Mercury snuck out of the cave. In the world outside, he discovered a tortoise shell. He added strings to the shell to create the first lyre. A lyre is a stringed instrument that looks similar to a small harp. Mercury traveled farther from the cave. Eventually he spotted some cows. The cows belonged to Apollo. Apollo was Mercury's older brother and the god of the Sun. Apollo was supposed to be guarding the cows, but he was nowhere to be seen.

Mercury thought it would be funny to steal them. But he needed to cover his tracks. Mercury padded the cattle's hooves and made them walk backwards. This would confuse the trail. Apollo would not know where to look. Mercury sacrificed two of the cows to the Olympic gods to thank them for his good fortune. He then hid the rest in a cave and crawled back into his cave with his mother.

Apollo returned to find his cattle
missing. He looked all over the world
for them. But he couldn't find them
anywhere. Some stories say Apollo
used his ability to see into the future
to find where they had gone.
His visions led him straight to
Mercury. Apollo accused Mercury
of stealing his cattle, but Mercury
claimed he didn't do it. Apollo
approached their father, Jupiter,
with his complaint.

Mercury was clever, but he
could not fool Jupiter. Jupiter was
amused by Mercury's cunning.
But he insisted that Mercury
return the cattle. Mercury led Apollo to the cave, where
Apollo soon discovered there were two cows missing.
Mercury quietly began playing his special lyre. Apollo was
also the god of music, so the new instrument fascinated

THE TWELVE TABLES

Ancient Romans engraved their
laws on tablets for everyone to
read. They called these laws
the Twelve Tables. Thievery was
included on the tablets. The
tablets stated that if a thief was
caught stealing, he or she may be
executed. Ancient Romans thought
Mercury brought good fortune.
To protect their homes against
thieves, some ancient Romans
placed wooden posts of Mercury
at the entrances.

him. He listened to the beautiful music and completely forgot about his missing cattle. In the end, Apollo loved the lyre so much that he traded Mercury his entire herd of cattle for it. The brothers became great friends. But it's not surprising that Mercury went on to become the god of thieves and trickery.

As Mercury grew, so did his skills of trickery and thievery. He was known for stealing objects from the other gods. He stole Apollo's bow and arrows, Vulcan's tools, and even Neptune's trident. Mercury thought about taking Jupiter's famous thunderbolts, but he was afraid of getting burned.

Mercury used his cunning for much more than thievery and tricks. He is credited with many inventions that helped mankind. Some believe Mercury helped create the alphabet. Ancient Romans even believed he created language, writing, and the musical scale. Mercury was worshiped throughout Rome as the god of literature, public speaking, and as a patron of poetry.

Mercury was also the patron god of athletes. According to ancient Romans, he invented boxing, wrestling, footraces, and gymnastics. Gymnasiums throughout Rome bore Mercury's name and image. Many festivals and athletic contests were held in his honor.

ROMAN ALPHABET
The Romans adapted their alphabet from the ancient Greeks. It is believed Mercury came up with the idea of letters. He thought of them while watching cranes fly in the sky. Their bodies and wings created forms when they flew, such as the letter W. Most of these ancient letters are the same ones the English language uses today.

Another of Mercury's many skills was his ability to keep secrets. Humans and gods, including his father, trusted him with messages. Jupiter decided to make Mercury the messenger and dealmaker of the gods. He gave Mercury gifts that would help him perform his job. Jupiter gave him a pair of sandals and a cap. Both had wings. These allowed Mercury to travel at the speed of light. Apollo gave Mercury a staff called the caduceus. The staff had two snakes wrapping around it and was sometimes depicted with wings at the top. With these tools, Mercury was ready to undertake missions for the gods.

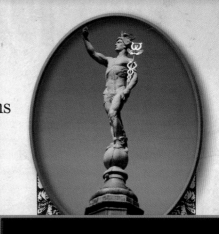

ROMAN ROADS
Ancient Romans had a saying, "All roads lead to Rome." The city was considered the center of the empire. As such, every city and province had to be connected to Rome. Romans built their roads in straight lines. They used stone bridges and tunnels if necessary. Mercury was the patron of roads and travelers, so Romans often placed statues of him at crossways or over roads.

Between solving problems and carrying messages, Mercury knew just about everything that was happening in the mythical world. He had a kind heart. Mercury always tried to solve problems. He wanted the outcome to be good for everyone. He was the best dealmaker in the world. Mercury became associated with any gain, honest or otherwise. His titles included the god of trade and commerce. Mortals who came upon any sort of luck thought it was the work of Mercury. They thought if they found a treasure it was surely a gift from the god.

Mercury was already a busy god. But he was tasked with another job. He was also the conductor of the dead. It was Mercury's role to escort the souls of the dead to the underworld. He brought them to the River Styx. This river ran past the entrance to the underworld. There, he turned the souls over to Charon. Charon was the ferryman for Pluto, the god of the dead. Charon took the souls from Mercury and transported them down the river to the underworld.

Mercury was one of few gods who could enter and leave the underworld without consequences. Most gods who entered the underworld were not allowed back out. The Olympic gods knew that Mercury was a trickster, but they still trusted him. He was both cunning and intelligent, so most of Mercury's missions were successful.

Mercury served as Jupiter's personal messenger and agent. Because of this, Mercury's most notable adventures involved Jupiter. During one of these adventures, Jupiter wanted to test humans. He asked Mercury to come with him to Earth. The two gods disguised themselves as human travelers. But no one offered them a place to stay. Only one couple gave them shelter. The gods rewarded these two for their kindness. They turned the couple's small cottage into a magnificent temple.

Jupiter also asked Mercury to help him hide secrets from Juno. Jupiter changed the maiden Io into a cow to keep their relationship a secret. Jupiter then gave the cow to Juno as a gift to try to protect Io. But Juno was suspicious. She sent Argus to guard Io the cow. Argus was a monster with 100 eyes.

Jupiter was distraught. But Mercury was clever. He came up with a plan to free Io. Mercury disguised himself as a shepherd. He went to Argus and began playing soft music with his lyre. He then told a long and boring tale. Argus slowly fell asleep. Mercury touched each of Argus's 100 eyes with his magic staff so that he would sleep forever.

Another of Mercury's adventures involved the hero Perseus. Perseus was on a mission to collect the head of Medusa. Medusa was a hideous, snake-haired monster called a Gorgon. She could turn men to stone with just her gaze.

Perseus thought the mission was impossible. Jupiter took pity on him. He asked Minerva and Mercury to help Perseus. Minerva lent Perseus her bronze shield. It was as shiny as a mirror. Minerva told him to use it to see Medusa's reflection so he wouldn't be turned to stone. Mercury gave him a sword that was sharp enough to cut stone.

Even with these tools, Perseus needed more help. Mercury flew him to see the Gray sisters. The sisters were ancient sea spirits. Gray-haired from birth, they only had one eye and tooth, which they had to share. Perseus stole their eye and tooth. To earn them back, the sisters agreed to help Perseus defeat Medusa. They gave him winged sandals, a cap of invisibility, and a magic bag. Mercury then pointed Perseus in the direction of the island of the Gorgon. With the god's help, Perseus succeeded in his quest.

Between missions, Mercury fell in love with many beautiful maidens. He never married. But he did have several children. One of his sons was Faunus. Faunus was born with the legs of a goat. He also had pointed ears and small horns. His lower body was covered in dark, shaggy fur.

Faunus's mother thought he was hideous. But Mercury loved his funny-looking boy. He brought Faunus with him to Mount Olympus. Faunus amused the gods. He quickly won their hearts. When he returned to Earth, the gods placed him in charge of nature. Faunus was a moody and noisy god. He enjoyed music just like his father. He also invented an instrument. He played his panpipes as he chased nymphs through the woods.

Autolycus was another of Mercury's sons. His mother was Chione. Mercury touched the beautiful nymph with his wand and made her fall asleep. She bore Autolycus. This son inherited his father's thievery skills. Autolycus was able to change the shape of anything he stole. He could then make it and himself invisible. He was so good at stealing that he became the most famous thief in all of ancient times.

Ancient Romans honored Mercury as the god of trade and merchants. He was commonly identified with Hermes, the Greek messenger of the gods. Mercury is most often shown wearing his famous winged sandals and cap. Artists also show him carrying his caduceus. This staff was said to have the power to join people who were divided by conflict. Mercury was usually shown as a handsome, beardless, youthful god.

Mercury is often a supporting character in Roman myths. But he appears in more myths than any other god of ancient Rome. Mercury was a favorite of both Roman storytellers and audiences. His mischief and trickery made for entertaining stories.

MERCURY THE PLANET
The planet Mercury is named after the Roman god. Mercury was also the god of astronomy and astrology. Mercury is the smallest planet in our solar system. It is the planet closest to the Sun. It is often referred to as the morning star. It is visible without a telescope.

Since the Roman god Mercury and the Greek god Hermes were very similar, many of their myths combined. But some stories about Mercury were distinctly Roman. For instance, in Rome he became the god of trade, thieves, and travel. A temple was dedicated to Mercury in 495 BC.

Mercury's birthday was considered to be May 15. For good luck, the Romans celebrated a festival that day each year. The festival was known as Mercuralia. There was a fountain in Rome known as Aqua Mercurii. During the festival, merchants sprinkled their merchandise, ships, and heads with water from that fountain. They offered prayers to Mercury. They asked Mercury for profit, forgiveness of past and future offenses, and the continued ability to cheat customers.

CIRCUS MAXIMUS

The Circus Maximus was the largest Roman horse-racing stadium. It was constructed during the 6th century BC. It was originally built of wood and burnt down twice. The Romans rebuilt it using concrete and marble. Attendance in the stadium was free and open to everyone. The arena also served as a major center of commerce. Its location next to Mercury's temple was fitting, since Mercury was the god of profit and trade. Only the ruins remain today.

Mercury was a god of many talents. He brought a sense of humor to Mount Olympus, such as when he stole Apollo's bow and Neptune's trident. But he was also responsible, trustworthy, clever, and cunning. Mercury remains a favorite in Roman mythology.

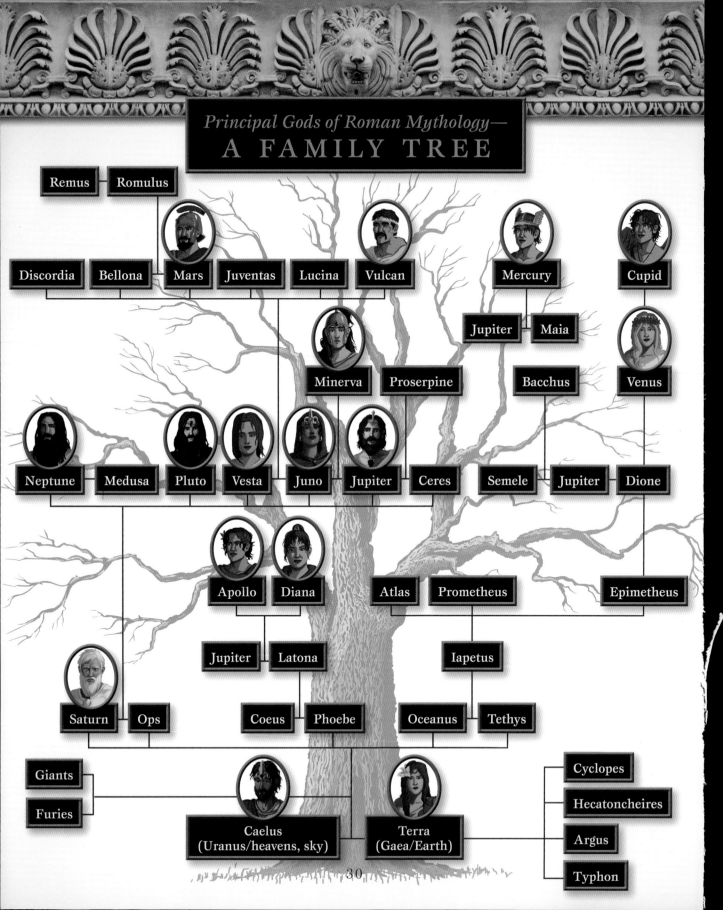

Principal Gods of Roman Mythology—
A FAMILY TREE

Remus — Romulus

Discordia — Bellona — Mars — Juventas — Lucina — Vulcan — Mercury — Cupid

Jupiter — Maia

Minerva — Proserpine — Bacchus — Venus

Neptune — Medusa — Pluto — Vesta — Juno — Jupiter — Ceres — Semele — Jupiter — Dione

Apollo — Diana — Atlas — Prometheus — Epimetheus

Jupiter — Latona — Iapetus

Coeus — Phoebe — Oceanus — Tethys

Saturn — Ops

Giants

Furies

Caelus
(Uranus/heavens, sky)

Terra
(Gaea/Earth)

Cyclopes

Hecatoncheires

Argus

Typhon

THE GREEK GODS

Ancient Greeks believed gods and goddesses ruled the world. The gods fell in love and struggled for power, but they never died. The ancient Greeks believed their gods were immortal. The Greek people worshiped the gods in temples. They felt the gods would protect and guide them. Over time, the Romans and many other cultures adopted the Greek myths as their own. While these other cultures changed the names of the gods, many of the stories remain the same.

SATURN: *Cronus*
God of Time and God of Sowing
Symbol: Sickle or Scythe

JUPITER: *Zeus*
King of the Gods, God of Sky, Rain, and Thunder
Symbols: Thunderbolt, Eagle, and Oak Tree

JUNO: *Hera*
Queen of the Gods, Goddess of Marriage,
  Pregnancy, and Childbirth
Symbols: Peacock, Cow, and Diadem
  (Diamond Crown)

NEPTUNE: *Poseidon*
God of the Sea
Symbols: Trident, Horse, and Dolphin

PLUTO: *Hades*
God of the Underworld
Symbols: Invisibility Helmet and Pomegranate

MINERVA: *Athena*
Goddess of Wisdom, War, and Arts and Crafts
Symbols: Owl, Shield, Loom, and Olive Tree

MARS: *Ares*
God of War
Symbols: Wild Boar, Vulture, and Dog

DIANA: *Artemis*
Goddess of the Moon and Hunt
Symbols: Deer, Moon, and Silver Bow and Arrows

APOLLO: *Apollo*
God of the Sun, Music, Healing, and Prophecy
Symbols: Laurel Tree, Lyre, Bow, and Raven

VENUS: *Aphrodite*
Goddess of Love and Beauty
Symbols: Dove, Swan, and Rose

CUPID: *Eros*
God of Love
Symbols: Bow and Arrows

MERCURY: *Hermes*
Messenger to the Gods, God of Travelers and Trade
Symbols: Crane, Caduceus, Winged Sandals,
  and Helmet

FURTHER INFORMATION

BOOKS

Allan, Tony. *Exploring the Life, Myth, and Art of Ancient Rome*. New York: Rosen Publishing, 2012.

Mincks, Margaret. *What We Get from Roman Mythology*. Ann Arbor, MI: Cherry Lake Publishing, 2015.

Temple, Teri. *Hermes: God of Travels and Trade*. Mankato, MN: Child's World, 2013.

WEB SITES

Visit our Web site for links about Mercury: *childsworld.com/links*

Note to Parents, Teachers, and Librarians: We routinely verify our Web links to make sure they are safe and active sites. So encourage your readers to check them out!

INDEX